Gargoylz

Ride to the Rescue

Gargoylz: grotesque stone
creatures found on old
buildings, spouting rainwater
from the guttering.
Sometimes seen causing
mischief and mayhem
before scampering away
over rooftops.

www.kidsatrandomhouse.co.uk

Read all the
Gargoylz adventures!

Gargoylz

Ride to the Rescue

Burchett & Vogler
illustrated by Leighton Noyes
RED FOX

GARGOYLZ GARGOYLZ RIDE TO THE RESCUE

A RED FOX BOOK 978 1 849 41080 9

First published in Great Britain by Red Fox,
an imprint of Random House Children's Books
A Random House Group Company

This edition published 2010

1 3 5 7 9 10 8 6 4 2

Series created and developed by Amber Caravéo

The Random House Group Limited supports the Forest Stewardship Council
(FSC), the leading international forest certification organization. All our titles
that are printed on Greenpeace-approved FSC-certified paper carry the FSC
logo. Our paper procurement policy can be found at
www.rbooks.co.uk/environment

 **Mixed Sources**
Product group from well-managed
forests and other controlled sources
FSC   www.fsc.org Cert no. TT-COC-2139
© 1996 Forest Stewardship Council

Set in Bembo Schoolbook

Red Fox Books are published by Random House Children's Books,
61–63 Uxbridge Road, London W5 5SA

www.**kids**at**randomhouse**.co.uk
www.**rbooks**.co.uk

Addresses for companies within The Random House Group Limited can be
found at: www.randomhouse.co.uk/offices.htm

THE RANDOM HOUSE GROUP Limited Reg. No. 954009

A CIP catalogue record for this book is available from the British Library.

Printed and bound in Great Britain by CPI Bookmarque, Croydon, CR0 4TD

For Danielle Finch – a very special Gargoylz fan
- **Burchett & Vogler**

For Olivia, with love x
- **Leighton Noyes**

Hello, I'm the Web Gargoyle.
Look out for me – I'll be hiding in one
of the pictures in the book.
When you spot me, be sure to make a
note of the secret codeword I'm holding.
The codeword unlocks a secret level
of the amazing Gargoylz game
on our fabulous website at
www.gargolyz.co.uk

Oldacre Primary School

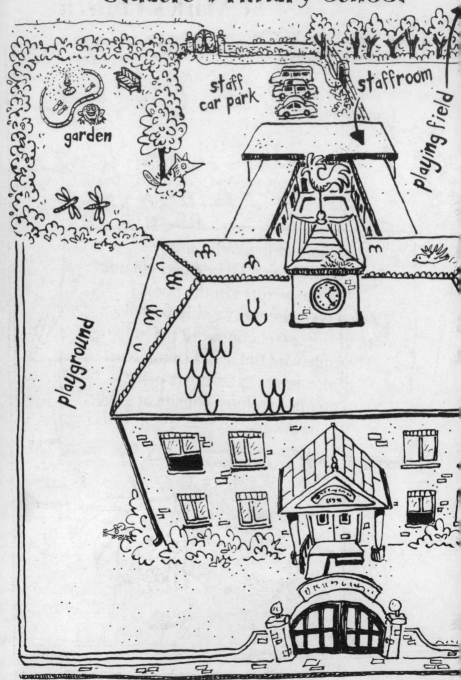

St Mark's Church

little butterfly fluttering about

School Report - Max Black

Days absent: 0

Days late: 0

Max is never afraid to make a contribution to history lessons. His demonstration of a battering ram using a broom and a bucket was very realistic, although the resulting hole in the classroom door was not ideal.

I worry that Max only seems to play with Ben Neal, but he assures me he has a lot of friends at the local church.

Class teacher - Miss Deirdre Bleet

Max Black's behaviour this term has been outrageous. He has repeatedly broken school rule number 739: boys must not tell 'knock knock' jokes in assembly. He is still playing pranks with Ben Neal. Mrs Pumpkin is absent again after the exploding paint pot incident. And Mrs Simmer, the head dinner lady, says the mincing machine has never been the same since he fed his maths test into it.

Head teacher - Hagatha Hogsbottom (Mrs)

School Report - Ben Neal

Days absent: 0

Days late: 0

This term Ben has
been very inventive in PE.
However, attempting to tightrope-walk
across the hall was a little dangerous
- and used up all the skipping ropes.
He spends far too much time in class
looking out of the window and waving at
the gravestones in the churchyard. He
would be better learning his spellings - a
word he insists on writing as 'spellingz'.

Class teacher - Miss Deirdre Bleet

Ben Neal is always polite, but I am deeply concerned
about his rucksack. It often looks very full - and
not with school books, I am certain. It has sometimes
been seen to wriggle and squirm. I suspect that he
is keeping a pet in there. If so, it is outrageous and
there will be trouble.

Head teacher - Hagatha Hogsbottom (Mrs)

Contents

1. Castle Chaos

"I can't wait till we get to Barebones Castle," exclaimed Max Black. "It's going to be an awesome day out."

"And I can't wait for the medieval fight this afternoon," said his best friend, Ben Neal, peering out of the car window to catch his first glimpse of the castle. "It's knights on horses poking each other with long sticks!"

Ben's mum laughed. "It's called a joust," she told him. She was sitting in the front of the car, map reading for Mrs Black. Max and Ben were sitting in the folding seats at the very back with the picnic.

"You're so silly, Ben," his big sister, Arabella, piped up from the seat in front of them. "Fancy not knowing what a joust is."

"So silly," echoed Jessica, Max's five-year-old sister.

"Never mind the fighting," said Arabella. "What's more important is there'll be people in medieval costumes and they'll show us what life was like hundreds of years ago. It will be very interesting."

"Very interesting," chanted Jessica.

"There's only one thing spoiling today, Agent Neal," whispered Max. "Those two

2

gruesome girls had to come with us."

"They should have stayed at home, Agent Black," agreed Ben. "Castles aren't for scaredy-cats like them. They're for superspies like us."

"And Jessica's always copying everything Arabella does," muttered Max. "She told Mum that when she's eleven she wants to be just like Arabella."

"But why does she have to start practising now?" groaned Ben.

"Look at her. She's got a pink hair band like Arabella . . ." said Max.

"And she giggles like Arabella," added Ben.

"And now she's even sniffing like Arabella," Max sighed.

"Two Arabellas," said Ben, pulling his hair in desperation.

"It's the worst nightmare in the history of worst nightmares."

"I hope our picnic's healthy," came Arabella's voice.

"I hope so too," said Jessica.

"I only eat healthy food," Arabella went on, "like vegetables."

"Ooh, I love vegetables," said Jessica.

"That's not true!" Max whispered to Ben. "Jess eats about one carrot a month — and then only if Mum makes her. If she had her way, she'd eat sweets for every meal."

But Ben wasn't listening. He was gawping at the plastic cool bag wedged between them. "There's something alive in there," he gasped. "I saw the lid move."

Max peered at the bag.

"Maybe it's a snake," he said hopefully. "Or a rat."

He slowly opened the top.

"Greetingz!" came a growly purr, and a pair of golden eyes twinkled out of the darkness.

Max's spy radar burst into life: small, stone-coloured, and with a mischievous monkey face. Max knew what that meant. It was Toby, codename: Gargoyle Friend.

"Cool!" exclaimed Ben. "Who cares about stupid sisters when we've got Toby with us? This trip's going to be awesome after all!"

Toby and the other gargoylz lived on the church next to the boys' school. Everyone else thought they were just ugly old statues but Max and Ben knew better. The little stone creatures were alive and loved to play tricks as much as the boys.

"Are we there yet?" came a chirpy voice from the picnic basket at Ben's feet.

He flung it open. A gargoyle with a long snout was sitting on the bags of crisps.

"You're here too, Neb," whispered Ben in delight.

"So's Barney," answered Neb in a low voice. "He's busy eating the cookiez."

"I've finished them all!" A doggy face appeared, covered in crumbs.

It was Barney, wedged between the muffins and the jammy dodgers. "I'm so full I can feel a smell coming on," he said.

"Don't do it in the car," gasped Toby. "Too pongy!"

Not only did the gargoylz like to play tricks, they all had their own special powers as well. Barney could make the most amazing bottom-burp smells. The problem was, he couldn't always control them!

Max peered into the cool bag. "I hope no one's had the sausage rolls," he said. "They're my favourite."

He had just picked up a handful of sandwiches to check underneath, when Arabella's face appeared between the headrests. Jessica popped up next to her.

Neb used his special power to change colour so that he blended into the background like a chameleon, and Toby and Barney hid under the seats.

"Are you starting on the picnic?" demanded Arabella.

"How naughty!" Jessica piped up.

"You've eaten all the cookies!" snapped Arabella, peering into the basket.

"Every single one!" gasped Jessica.

"*We* didn't eat them," protested Max.

"Yes we did," said Ben quickly. He nudged Max. "We can't tell them who really ate them!" he muttered.

"Er . . . OK, yes, we did eat them," stammered Max.

"Greedy boys," said Arabella. "I'm telling Mum."

"So am I," added Jessica.

"But you said you

were only going to eat healthy food," said
Ben, "so you wouldn't have wanted any
cookies anyway!"

Arabella glared at them. Then she
sniffed and turned away. Jessica did the
same. "OK, I'll let you off this time,"
Arabella said over her shoulder.

"Clever answer, Agent Neal,"
whispered Max.

Toby and Barney crept out from
their hiding places, and Neb stopped
looking like the picnic basket
and changed back to his
usual stony colour.

"Sorry," said
Barney sheepishly.
"I didn't mean
to eat all the
cookiez. They
just sort of
jumped into
my mouth."

At that moment the car swung round a
corner and the castle came into view.
It was huge, with four tall turrets and
long red and gold banners hanging
down from the battlements.

Toby pressed his nose against the window. "It's much bigger than Saint Mark's Church," he said, eyes wide with amazement.

"You'll love it, gargoylz," Max told them. "There are knights and a moat – and even a torture chamber."

"They used to have torture chambers when we were young," said Barney nervously. "Nasty places."

"That was hundreds of years ago," Ben assured him. "They don't use them any more. It's just a really cool bunch of gory pokers and thumbscrews and all that sort of thing."

"Can't wait!" declared Neb in excitement.

"We've got a problem, though," said Max, scratching his head. "How do we get the gargoylz out of the car without anyone seeing them?"

"Got it!" said Ben. "Secret plan: Distract Everyone."

"Brilliant!" answered Max. "Then the gargoylz can make their getaway!"

"Now it is time for one of my smellz!" said Barney. "No one will stay in the car after that!"

Max and Ben made a face at each other. "We'll have to use our superspy nose clamps," said Max. "Codename: Fingers."

The car pulled into a parking space. Barney's eyes glazed over and the next second a dreadful pong filled the air. It was like the smelliest rotten eggs in the world. Max and Ben pinched their noses hard.

"Oh, boys!" groaned Ben's mum,
flinging open the door.

"Everyone out!" gasped Max's mum.
She handed Max the keys. "Once that
smell has gone from my car, lock up and
come and join us."

"Stinkpots!" said Arabella, diving out
of the car and making for the castle
entrance.

"Stinky stinkpots!" shrieked Jessica,
close behind her.

As soon as they'd all gone, Ben opened
his door to let the gargoylz out. "Good
trick!" he spluttered, flapping the smell
away with a paper plate.

"See you later!" whispered Toby.
He and Neb scuttled off into the bushes.

"One more gargoyle
to go," called Barney
mysteriously as he
scampered after
the others.

"One more?" said Max, looking around in amazement. "I can't see anyone else."

They searched among the picnic things.

"Barney must have been tricking us," said Ben, pulling out a rolled-up picnic blanket and flopping down on it. "There are no other gargoylz here."

To his surprise the blanket snorted! Ben shot to his feet. The boys quickly pulled at the corners, unrolling the blanket, and a lumpy, troll-like gargoyle fell out.

"Rufus!" exclaimed Ben. "That blanket was a mega-good hiding place!"

"And it kept Barney's smell away," said Rufus, sitting up dizzily.

He got to his feet and staggered after his friends,

a cheeky grin on his huge, warty face.

"Secret plan successful!" declared Max.

"Castle, here we come!" yelled Ben.

They bounded across the drawbridge over the moat. Their mums were buying tickets from a man dressed like an olden days guard.

"This castle is so cool!" said Ben, examining the map on the wall. "Where shall we go first? The torture chamber or the battlements?"

"Queen's bedchamber!" said Arabella firmly.

"Queen's bedchamber," repeated Jessica-the-Echo. "There might be some pretty princess clothes there."

"And we'll all go together," said Ben's mum, paying the cashier. "We can't trust you two boys to behave on your own after that nasty smelly trick."

Max and Ben groaned as they trailed up the main staircase.

"Why would anyone want to look

at clothes when there are instruments of
torture to play with?" whispered Max.
"Mothers are as bad as girls sometimes."

Arabella let out a shriek of delight
when she saw the long robes displayed on
models around the royal four-poster bed.
Jessica cried out too.

A woman in medieval costume came
forward and curtsied. She pointed to a
long rack of brightly coloured clothes.

"I am your humble servant, young mistresses," she said. "Allow me to help you dress up."

The girls shrieked again.

The boys gawped at each other. "Get back against the wall," said Ben quickly. "We don't want to get dressed up!"

"Look at me!" trilled Jessica as the servant put a tall pointy hat with a long flowing veil on her head.

Once she'd helped both Jessica and Arabella dress like medieval princesses, the servant curtsied again. "I will leave you now, my ladies. I have others to attend to," she said, and left the room.

The mums cooed and took
photographs as Arabella paraded around
the room in a trailing gown, with Jessica
following behind in her princess
hat and velvet cloak.
The boys
slumped in a
corner.
"This is
so boring!"
moaned Max.
"There's not
even a suit of
armour to try on. How do we escape,
Agent Neal?"

To his surprise Ben was grinning. "Help
is at hand, Agent Black," he whispered.

Max heard Toby's growly chuckle
coming from the costume rack. The next
minute a long red dress began to jiggle
on its hanger! Luckily Mrs Black and
Mrs Neal were too busy examining their

photos of the girls to notice.

The boys watched eagerly as Arabella swept over to change outfits, followed by her faithful shadow, Jessica. The red dress suddenly flapped a sleeve under their noses. The two girls screamed in horror and ran off to hide behind the bed. Then a glove rose up from the shelf and waved at them. The boys could just see the outline of Neb with the glove on the end of his nose. They heard Barney doing his best ghostly wail from the hat stand.

"There are ghosts in the clothes!" squealed Arabella.

"Ghosts!" echoed Jessica in terror.

Max and Ben stuffed their fists in their

mouths to stop themselves snorting with laughter.

"You're imagining things!" declared Max's mum, steering the trembling girls out of the room. "Clothes can't be haunted!"

"Was that another of your tricks, boys?" asked Mrs Neal suspiciously.

"Not us," said Max as they followed them into the corridor. "We were miles away."

Arabella glanced fearfully back over her shoulder.

So did Jessica.

A pair of shoes began to tap dance on the floor. A white petticoat was bouncing around them, followed by a lacy blouse, two hats and a pair of bloomers.

The girls shrieked, and scuttled off down the staircase. Max and Ben caught up with them at the bottom.

"I wouldn't go near that room again, girls," advised Max, trying to keep a straight face.

"The gruesome ghosts of the wardrobe live there," warned Ben. "You might feel a shiver in your shirt."

"Or a spook in your skirt," said Max.

"Or a phantom in your pants," added Ben helpfully.

"We'll go to the kitchen instead,"
quavered Arabella.

"Pots and pans aren't haunted," said
Jessica.

"Good idea," said Ben's mum in relief.

Max and Ben groaned. "Do we have
to come?" Ben asked. "We want to go to
the dungeon. It's more fun than stupid
cooking."

"We were good in the queen's
bedchamber," Max pointed out.

"All right then," said his mum. "But
make sure you behave yourselves."

"*Us?*" said Max, looking shocked.

"We always behave
ourselves," said Ben.

Before their mothers
could reply, they
raced off down
the stone steps
that led to
the dungeon.

"This is so cool!" exclaimed Max as they
wandered among the rusty old pliers
and thumbscrews in the gloomy torture
chamber. Grim-looking models stood
around holding chains and spikes, and the
ancient walls were lit by lamps that looked
like flickering candles. Every so often blobs
of red slime slid down the walls.

"It looks just like blood," gasped Ben. "I hope the gargoylz get here soon. They'll love it."

"Here's the rack!" said Max eagerly. He led the way to a huge wooden frame with a ragged figure tied to it by his hands and feet. "I bet those medieval people ended up really tall after they'd been stretched on here. They'd have been really good at basketball."

"What's this?" asked Ben, stopping at a long metal cabinet that was standing against a wall. "It looks like the sort of case you'd find an Egyptian mummy in."

Max read the label. *"Iron Maiden.*

Prisoners were shut in here and spiked to death."

"Gruesome!" said Ben, fiddling with the lock. "Let's open it. There might still be someone full of holes inside."

"Shouldn't think so," Max began. "No one gets spiked nowadays—"

Ben flung open the case and the boys jumped back in astonishment. The iron maiden wasn't empty! A stone-coloured, warty creature was standing inside, grinning at them.

"Rufus!" gasped Ben. "What are you doing in there?"

"I was having a doze," Rufus answered with a grin.

"Don't the spikes hurt?" asked Max.

Rufus shook his head. "I'm smaller than humanz – too small for the spikes to reach me," he assured them.

Just then they heard the ghastly chatter
of girly voices.

"It's our sisters!" groaned Max. "So our
mums won't be far behind."

"They're coming this way," added Ben
urgently. "They'll see Rufus!"

Max swung the heavy case shut just as
the girls appeared, he and Ben hurriedly
stood in front of it.

"Mum says you have to meet us
outside for the picnic in one hour," said
Arabella, giving a shiver as she
glanced around.

"One hour precisely,"
added Jessica, wagging her
finger.

"See you later then,"
said Max, trying to
shoo them away.

Arabella peered hard
at the boys. "You look

guilty," she said suspiciously. "What have you been up to?"

"Nothing," said Ben, putting on his wide-eyed, innocent look. It always worked with the dinner ladies at school, who gave him extra waffles. It *never* worked with his sister.

"What's that thing behind you?" she demanded.

"We want to know!" insisted Jessica, trying to push past.

"It's a nasty iron maiden," Max said desperately. He had to stop them seeing Rufus. "You wouldn't like it."

"Oh yes we would," said Arabella. "An iron maiden doesn't sound nasty at all."

"It is," said Ben. "Honest."

Arabella snorted.

"I don't believe you. Get out of the way."

"Yes, get out of the way!" said Jessica-the-Echo.

Max and Ben held their breath as Arabella heaved the metal case open. The door swung back with a clang – revealing a pale, grinning skeleton!

It lolled in the iron maiden with long, dangling limbs and dead eyes that stared straight at the girls. Rufus had used his special power and had turned into a terrifying pile of bones.

Arabella let out an ear-splitting shriek that bounced around the walls

of the dungeon. So did Jessica. Max and
Ben clapped their hands over their ears.
The girls turned and collided with their
mothers. They screeched again and fled up
the stone staircase.

"It wasn't us," Max called to his mum.
"They just saw a silly skeleton."

"We did tell them not to look, Agent
Black," said Ben sympathetically as their
mums disappeared after the girls.

"It's not our fault they didn't listen,
Agent Neal," agreed Max, shaking his
head. "Well done, Rufus!"

Rufus stepped out of the iron maiden
and took a bow. "That was my best

performance yet!" he declared as he shrank back into his stony form.

The other gargoylz came scuttling out from behind a metal cage.

"We saw it all," said Barney.

"I haven't laughed so much since Neb sniffed up a bunch of grapes and pelted the vicar with pips," chuckled Toby.

Ben rubbed his hands together. "Now our scaredy-cat sisters have gone, we've got the whole castle to explore."

"What are we waiting for?" cried Max. "Let's have a medieval spy adventure!"

2. New Friendz

Max and Ben and the gargoylz crept
around the dungeons, pretending to be
medieval spies. At last they came to a
shadowy doorway where stone steps led
up into the darkness.

"A creepy staircase," gasped Ben.
"Awesome!"

"I wonder where it goes," said Max.

"There's a sign!" called Toby excitedly.
"It says **TO THE BATTLEMENTS**."

"We could have some fun on the roof,"
Max suggested. "There might be cannons.
Follow me, everyone!"

He charged up the spiral steps, Ben
and the gargoylz hard on his heels. At last
they came to an open door. There was a
rope strung across with a big notice on it:
CLOSED FOR CLEANING.

"Does that mean we can't go through?"
asked Barney, looking disappointed.

"I think it's OK," said
Ben, peering through the
doorway. "There isn't
any cleaning going on
at the moment."

"Excellent," Max
grinned. "But we'd
better check the
area's clear of enemy
agents. We don't want
to be attacked by a load
of medieval cleaners with
scrubbing brushes."

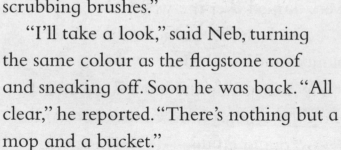

"I'll take a look," said Neb, turning
the same colour as the flagstone roof
and sneaking off. Soon he was back. "All
clear," he reported. "There's nothing but a
mop and a bucket."

"That's not very medieval," said Ben
as they emerged into the sunshine.

The flat roof was bounded on all four
sides by the battlements. The ends of the

banners they'd seen from the car park were draped over the walls.

"This is nearly as big as the school playground," said Max.

"Where are the cannonz?" asked Toby.

"I thought there'd be bowz and arrowz," said Rufus.

"And catapults," added Barney.

"Don't worry," Max told them. "We can pretend we've got all the weapons we need for a really awesome game."

"Good thinking, Agent Black," said
Ben, his eyes lighting up. "Come on,
gargoylz. Our castle's under attack."

"And the bucket's full of burning oil,"
agreed Max, "ready to pour on top of
an invading army."

Ben grabbed the mop. "This is the
sharpest spear in the history of sharpest
spears."

"I'll keep a lookout for enemies,"
declared Rufus, peering over the wall.

"Spluttering gutterz! This is a lot higher than our church at home."

Everyone ran over to join him. "Army approaching," announced Max, pointing at a group of tourists who were pouring

off a coach in the distant car park.

"They're coming this way, men!" shouted Ben.

"I'll get the oil," said Toby, grabbing the bucket. Cold, dirty water sploshed about inside.

"Help me load the cannon, Barney," yelled Ben, pretending he was rolling a heavy cannonball across the roof. Spines quivering with excitement, Barney scampered over to help him.

"We'll be the archers, won't we, Neb?" said Max, taking up his position by the wall. "We'll fire one hundred arrows a second ... Enemy coming closer."

The coach party was now streaming over the drawbridge.

"Get the cannon ready!" bellowed Ben. Barney and Rufus lifted the pretend cannonball and rolled it down the barrel

of the pretend cannon. "Stand back!" Ben
yelled as he pretented to light the fuse.

"*Boom!*" yelled Rufus.

Half the tourists were now lined up
waiting for tickets while the others were
in a queue for the toilets.

"Pour the burning oil over!" ordered
Max.

With Neb's help
Toby heaved the bucket
onto the battlements.
Then, before Max
and Ben could stop
them, they tipped
it over the edge
with a loud war
cry. Screams rose
from below as
cold, dirty water
splashed down
onto the
toilet queue.

"Uh-oh, hide!" hissed Max. They all ducked down out of sight, rolling around with laughter.

"Sorry!" chuckled Toby. "We forgot we were meant to be pretending."

Suddenly a gust of wheezing laughter burst out from behind one of the turrets.

Max, Ben and the gargoylz leaped up in alarm. Had they been discovered?

"What a magnificent jest!" said a rusty old voice, and a curious creature stepped out onto the roof.

Max's spy radar sprang into action: stone-coloured skin, feet and tail of a lion with the head and body of a human, pointy helmet. He knew what that meant: it was a gargoyle. But Max'd never seen a gargoyle like this before.

"He's very big,"

whispered Barney, hiding shyly behind Ben.

"And very old," said Toby. He gave a little bow. "Greetingz! We are the Saint Mark's Church gargoylz."

"Hail to ye," said the tall figure. He strode over to the boys and their friends. "It did my old stone good to see such a merry prank. I have not laughed so much since I dropped the king's under-breeches in the moat."

"That's old-fashioned talk for pants," said Neb with a giggle. "He dropped the king's pants in the moat."

"Awesome!" exclaimed Ben as his friends rocked with laughter.

The new gargoyle came over and prodded Max and Ben in the tummy. Then he held up

his paws in horror. "You are not made
of stone!" he cried. "You are humanz,
lurking among all these splendid gargoylz!
Humanz must not know I'm alive."

"It's all right," said Toby quickly. "These
boyz are special humanz. They're our
friendz and they like to play tricks, just
like gargoylz."

"They're much uglier than us, of
course," added Rufus.

The castle gargoyle nodded. "They
would frighten many a brave knight," he
said. "However, any friend of a gargoyle is
a friend of mine, no matter how gruesome.
But I forget my mannerz." He gave a deep
bow. "My name is Ethelstan. You may call
me Stan."

"I'm Max," said Max. He quickly introduced the others and they all bowed in turn.

"Are you the only gargoyle here, Stan?" asked Ben.

Their new friend shook his head. "Barebones Castle is swarming with us. We have lived here since it was built, nearly a thousand yearz ago." He put his hands to his mouth and gave a loud whistle.

A bunch of ancient and battered gargoylz scampered out from behind the turrets and over the battlements. They all wore odd bits of armour.

"We are the Barebones Brigade," said Stan proudly.

"Wow!" gasped Max. "I bet you lot have played some great tricks over the years."

The castle gargoylz looked sad. "We used to," Stan said with a sigh. "But no

one actually lives in the castle any more."

"Tell them about the time King William came to stay," called a chubby gargoyle in a breastplate.

"That is Egbert," Stan told them.

"You can call me Bert," said the gargoyle with a wave of his podgy paw.

"Indeed, Bert, that is a worthy tale," said Stan. The church gargoylz gathered round to listen. "William the Conqueror came here when the castle was first built and we heard that he was scared of earwigz."

"So we filled his boots with them!" added Bert. "We could hear his screamz from the top of the flagpole."

"That's a good

prank," said Barney.

The castle gargoylz also told tales of how they'd tucked a donkey up in the bishop's bed and fired Christmas puddings out of the cannon.

"The best one was when Queen Matilda sat in the butter," Stan finished.

"I put the dish on her throne," piped up a squeaky voice. "She slid all the way down the Great Hall on her buttery bottom!" A long-snouted gargoyle with sharp teeth scuttled out.

"This is Athelwolf," said Stan.

"Don't tell me," said Ben. "We can call him Wolf."

"How did you know?" gasped Stan, looking amazed.

Ben grinned. "Lucky guess."

Suddenly they heard heavy footsteps

on the stone stairs.

"Someone's coming!" gasped Toby and Stan together.

The Barebones Brigade froze in ugly poses along the battlements. The church gargoylz hopped up and turned to stone alongside them. Max and Ben hid behind the open door as a man in overalls appeared. He stared at the battlements and scratched his head.

"Huh!" he muttered to himself as he  spotted Toby, Barney, Neb and Rufus. "No one told me there'd be four new gargoylz arriving." He sniffed at Neb. "They're not very clean." He picked up the soggy mop and went to dunk it in the bucket. "Someone's nicked

me water!" he exclaimed, sticking his head
into the pail.

Max and Ben took their chance.
They leaped out of their hiding place
and beckoned to the church gargoylz
to follow. Then they gave the
Barebones Brigade a hasty
wave and charged off
down the stairs.

"That was a
nasty moment!"
said Rufus as they
collapsed in a heap
at the bottom.

"Not clean
indeed!" snorted
Neb. "Thanks to
my long squirty nose
I can give myself a shower every day!"

Max and Ben shuddered at the thought
of all that washing.

"He doesn't shower every day,"

whispered Barney. "He just sprayz the rest of us."

"Can we go back and see our new friendz again later?" asked Toby.

"Of course," agreed Ben. "But it's nearly picnic time now."

They ran back through the dungeons and up to ground level.

"This way," said Max, turning left. "I bet it's quicker."

They found themselves in a huge hall. There was no one else in sight.

All over the walls hung colourful shields covered in funny-looking lions and bears. Fearsome suits of armour stood in every corner. In the middle was a long table heaving with a delicious banquet. There were plates loaded with meat, bread and thick-crusted pies. Piles of pastries and tasty tarts were dotted around a model of the castle made out of marzipan. A whole roasted boar with a shiny red apple in its

mouth lay next to a stuffed peacock, its
magnificent tail fanned out over the table.

The gargoylz' eyes grew wide with
delight at all the food.

"Your mumz have made a delicious
feast," said Rufus, rushing towards the
table. "I'll start with a chicken leg."

"But this isn't our picnic," began Ben.
"It's . . ."

"And I'll have one of those piez with
the fish tailz poking out," said Neb, licking
his lips.

"None of this is . . ." Max tried to insist.
But their friends weren't listening.

"I'm still full from
all those cookiez,"
said Barney.

Then his eyes lit
up. "But perhaps
I could just
manage a nice,
juicy red apple."

He bounded onto the table and ploughed through the cakes and tarts, heading straight for the roast boar.

"Stop!" yelled the boys.

It was too late. Barney grabbed the apple from between the boar's teeth and bit down hard into it. There was a nasty cracking sound.

"Yuck!" spluttered Barney. "It tastes horrible."

Ben laughed. "That's because it isn't real! We tried to warn you. The whole feast is made of plastic."

The other gargoylz chuckled while Barney checked his stony teeth. "That's a relief," he said. "They're all still there. What a sneaky trick to play."

"It wasn't meant to be a trick," said Ben. "It's just to show visitors what people used to eat in the olden days."

"But it's given me an idea for a really good prank," said Max, his eyes twinkling. "There are more apples in this bowl."

He helped himself to two of the biggest ones and shoved them in his pockets. "We'll borrow these for a while."

"What's your plan, Agent Black?" asked Ben eagerly.

"Secret Plan: Picnic Surprise," said Max. "A little treat for our sisters, Agent Neal."

Ben grinned. "Apples are nice and healthy, Agent Black," he agreed. "Just the sort of food they love."

Max and Ben reached the picnic area as their mums and sisters were laying out the food. They paused to watch from behind a tree. The gargoylz goggled at the crisps, pork pies and sausage rolls appearing on the cloth.

"Can we join in?" asked Neb hopefully. "This is nearly as good as the feast inside."

Ben shook his head. "You'll be seen."

The gargoylz' faces fell.

"We'll save you some food," Max assured them.

Their little friends scampered happily off into the trees.

"I'll help," Max told his mother.

Mrs Black looked surprised to see him pile grapes and satsumas delicately onto a plate. But as soon as she'd gone to sit on her picnic chair, he whipped the plastic apples out of his pocket and plonked them on top.

Arabella suddenly whirled round and peered at the fruit. Jessica stretched out a hand towards it.

"No!" said Arabella sternly.

The boys looked at each other. Did Ben's sister suspect something?

She picked up a bowl of chopped vegetables. "Veg first," she told Jessica. "Fruit later."

She took two sticks of celery and half a carrot. So did her shadow.

The boys heaved sighs of relief and tucked into their pork pies.

"Disgusting!" sniffed Arabella, watching them chomp. "So unhealthy."

"Unhealthy!" echoed Jessica, trying to look as if she was enjoying her celery.

"It's lucky we're here then," said Max. "We can eat all the horrible yummy stuff you don't want."

Jessica stuck her tongue out at him.

Max and Ben polished off all the sausage rolls and cheesy footballs, washing them down with plenty of cola. Then they ate four cupcakes and three jammy dodgers and crammed their pockets full of goodies for the gargoylz.

Max winked at Ben. "Time for our secret plan, Agent Neal," he whispered.

Ben nodded. "Would you like a nice stodgy muffin, Arabella?" he asked.

"Certainly not!" she snapped. "I'm going to have some fruit."

"So am I!" said Jessica, looking longingly at the cakes.

Arabella dived for the satsumas.

"Our teacher, Miss Bleet, says that apples are the healthiest fruit of all," said Max quickly. "Shame there's only two. Do you want one, Ben?"

"Yum!" answered Ben.

Quick as a flash, the girls reached out, snatched the bright red apples and took the biggest bites they could.

A look of horror crossed their faces as their teeth crunched into the plastic.

"*Yow!*" yelped Arabella, throwing her apple into the bushes.

"*Double yow!*" cried Jessica, doing the same.

There was the sound of muffled, wheezy laughter from the nearest tree.

"It's not funny, boys!" protested Arabella. "You tricked us!"

"Time for a speedy getaway, Agent Neal," said Max.

The boys shot to their feet, gathered up the fake apples and ran off into the woods, ignoring their sisters' angry shouts.

As soon as they were out of sight, they stopped and high-fived.

"Secret Plan: Picnic Surprise was a huge success," said Max. "We'll put the apples back later."

The gargoylz came tumbling out of the trees.

"Where's our picnic?"

demanded Neb.

"Here it is . . ." The boys pulled out squashed sausage rolls, mangled muffins and squidgy sandwiches from their pockets.

The gargoylz' faces lit up and they pounced on the food.

"Spluttering gutterz!" said Toby, spraying everyone with crumbs. "This is what I call a feast!"

3. Sir Gargoyle!

As soon as the gargoylz had finished their secret picnic they joined Max and Ben, who were now exploring the woods of Barebones Castle.

"These are awesome trees for climbing," said Max, looking around.

"Dangling drainpipes!" exclaimed Rufus, taking hold of a sturdy branch. "This would make a better swing than the vicar's washing line!"

"Cool!" said Ben. He grabbed the branch and swung his legs.

But the gargoylz had frozen to the spot.

Then, quick as a flash, they scuttled up the trunk and disappeared.

"What's going on?" demanded Max.

"Humanz approaching!" came an invisible chorus from among the leaves.

A group of tall figures dressed from head to toe in shiny armour was striding along the path towards the boys. Each wore a different coloured feather in his

helmet. In the distance a loudspeaker
was calling all competitors to get ready
for the joust.

"Awesome!" exclaimed Ben as he
watched them pass. "They're the knights
who are going to take part in the contest."

"We'd better get going," said Max.
"We don't want to miss it."

The knights were out of sight now
so Rufus perched on the branch again.
"Just time for one swing," he said. "Watch
me, everyone. I'm Rufus the Amazing
Acrobat!" He did a wobbly handstand and
then swung round and round the branch
by his hands, getting faster and faster.

At that moment another knight came
scurrying into view, pulling on his
metal gloves.

Clang! Rufus's stony feet
whacked him right on the
head. The boys watched,
horrified, as the knight
staggered about, arms
whirling like a windmill.

Then he toppled over backwards into a bush and lay still, the red feather on his helmet quivering gently.

The boys and gargoylz dashed over to him.

"He spoiled my performance!" complained Rufus.

Barney peered into the knight's helmet. "His eyes are rolling around," he said. "Does that mean he's dead?"

"Of course not," said Toby. "I just heard him groan."

"I expect that was a snore," said Neb

brightly. "He's probably having a nap. The vicar does that after lunch on Sundayz."

"We could play a trick on him," said Barney. "Like we do to the vicar."

"Put stones in his socks," suggested Rufus.

"Or grass in his earz," said Toby eagerly.

"No tricks," Max told them firmly. "This knight is not having a nap. He's been knocked out."

"That's terrible," gasped Ben. "He's going to miss his turn in the contest."

The gargoylz looked shocked.

Just then they heard Ben's mum in the distance. "Come on, boys. You'll miss the jousting."

"What are we going to do, Agent Black?" hissed Ben. "We can't just leave him here."

"I don't know, Agent Neal." Max scratched his head. "Superspies don't often come across unconscious medieval knights."

"We'll look after him," promised Toby.

"And we'll make sure you see him in the joust," said Rufus.

"But how?" asked Ben.

"We'll do what the vicar does when old ladies faint in church," said Barney.

"What does he do?" Max wondered.

"He fanz them with a hymn book," replied Neb.

"Just the thing!" exclaimed Ben. "Thanks, gargoylz!"

The boys charged off in the direction of the jousting field.

Ben suddenly stopped and frowned.

"I've just had a thought," he said. "The gargoylz don't have a hymn book."

"Don't worry," Max told him. "They'll think of something."

"They'd better be quick," said Ben.

SECRET CODEWORD:
KING

"The joust's starting."

A great shout arose from the crowd as
Max and Ben joined their families on the
edge of the field. Two knights galloped
into the arena on gleaming white horses.
One had a purple feather in his helmet;

the other had a gold one. The knights
clanked their visors down over their faces,
tucked their long poles under their arms
and charged at each other from opposite
ends of the field. The crowds cheered and
whooped as the two knights charged
again and again, trying to knock each
other off their horses with long poles –
Ben's mum said they were called lances.

"Cool!" gasped Max. "We'll have to try
that in the playground."

"We could use our bikes as horses," said
Ben eagerly.

"And borrow the caretaker's brooms for
the poles," added Max.

At last the purple knight gave a cry
and fell off his horse. The gold knight
was the winner and galloped off to great
cheers.

"I hope the gargoylz have managed
to wake our knight up," said Max as two
more horses cantered into the arena.

Neither rider was wearing the red feather. Their battle was soon over, and more contestants took their place.

"We'd better go and make sure he's OK," whispered Max.

But the loudspeaker was now announcing the last fight. The crowd clapped and cheered, and the two knights appeared, ready to do battle.

"There he is!" gasped Max, pointing at a knight with a red feather in his helmet.

"Well done, gargoylz," cried Ben. "They

must have found something to flap at him
after all."

The red knight trotted past on his huge
stallion.

"He doesn't look quite right," Max
muttered to Ben. "His legs are all wobbly."

"He's probably a bit concussed still,"
said Ben. "That's what happens when
you get hit on the head and can't
remember anything."

"I hope he remembers what he's got to

do," said Max.

"Something's poking out of his helmet!" exclaimed Ben suddenly.

"That's Toby's tail!" gasped Max.

The boys stared hard into the visor.

"The rest of Toby's inside that helmet," whispered Max in astonishment.

"And Rufus is under the breastplate," added Ben. "I can just see his warts. Neb and Barney must be in there too. There's no knight in there at all. That armour's full of gargoylz!"

"Cool!" said Max.

"It's not cool." Ben's face was serious. "We've got to stop them."

"Why?" asked Max. "They'll have a great time. I wish I could have a go."

"But I bet they've never ridden a horse before," Ben pointed out, "or been in a jousting competition. They could get their stone chipped – or worse."

Max's face fell. "I hadn't thought of that." He sounded worried. "We don't want anything bad to happen to them."

The red knight was now facing his opponent – a fierce-looking rider with shining armour and a big black feather in his helmet. Max and Ben waved frantically at the gargoylz, but it was no good. The gargoyle knight just waved a floppy arm back at them as he took up his lance and began to charge.

Max and Ben covered their eyes.

"Look at the boys," sniggered Arabella.

"They don't dare watch the jousting."

"Cowardy custards!" chanted Jessica.

Max and Ben uncovered their eyes.

"We're not cowardy custards," said Ben.

He made himself look at the contest. The red knight was still on his horse — grimly clinging onto the reins with one hand and waving his lance around wildly with the other.

"Come on, red knight!" shouted Max. "You can do it . . . I hope!" he added under his breath as the two horses charged towards each other, hooves thundering.

"Come on, black knight!" shouted Arabella and Jessica immediately. "You're the best."

"Although I wish he had a pink feather," added Jessica.

The black knight had his lance aimed straight for the gargoylz' armour. Just in time, the red knight wobbled and swayed out of the way. The horses turned, ready for another charge. And then they were off again, hurtling towards each other.

The crowd yelled in excitement as the black knight aimed his lance right at the red knight's neck. Max and Ben went pale.

"It's too late for the garg— for him to duck this time," yelped Max.

But in an instant the Toby-filled helmet leaped off the knight's shoulders and the

lance plunged through empty air. The
crowd cheered and clapped wildly as the
red knight caught his own head.

"Clever trick!" one of the crowd
shouted.

"How did he do that?" yelled
someone else.

It was all too much for the poor black
knight. He raised his visor and gawped
in horror at his opponent, who was now
trotting round
the arena
with his head
tucked under
his arm.

"I've
knocked
his block
off!"

croaked the black knight. With that, he fell
from his horse in a dead faint and had to
be carried away to the first-aid tent.

"What a fantastic battle!" bellowed the loudspeaker. "Our winner is . . . the red knight! And he takes the prize for the best joust of the day!"

The gargoyle-filled knight did a very wobbly lap of honour around the arena, waving cheerily all the time. As soon as he'd finished and trotted off the field, Max and Ben slipped away from the crowd. They found the real red knight sitting on the grass where they'd left him, looking confused. The gargoylz had placed his armour beside him.

"What happened?" he groaned.

"You, er . . . walked into a branch and got knocked out," Max told him. "But you woke up and won your contest!"

"Did I?" asked the knight doubtfully. "I don't remember anything about it."

"You must have lost your memory," said Ben sympathetically.

"Have I?" said the red knight, scratching his head.

They heard the loudspeaker booming out from the field: "Calling the Red Knight. Would the Red Knight please come to collect his special prize."

"That's me!" gasped the knight. "So it must be true."

"Of course it is," said Max, helping him to his feet.

"You were very good."

"The best," said Ben, handing him his breastplate. "The crowd loved you."

"Why did I take my armour off?" asked the knight. "I expect you wanted to cool down when you'd finished," said Max quickly. "It must be very hot, all that charging about poking people with poles."

The knight nodded weakly, put his helmet over his head and straightened his feather. "Thanks for your help, boys," he croaked as they steered him into the field and up to the winners' stand. The crowd raised the loudest cheer of the day as the confused-looking red knight held up a gleaming gold cup.

"We must go and search out our fellow agents, the gargoylz," Max whispered to Ben.

The boys headed for the trees. As soon as they were out of sight of the crowds, four stony shapes jumped down in front of them.

"Well done, gargoylz," said Max. "You were awesome."

"I haven't had so much fun since we rode the vicar's bike into the pond," declared Toby.

"You're the ones who deserve the jousting cup," said Ben. "You saved the day!"

4. Toby in Danger

Max and Ben were in a hurry. They
had to get to the castle battlements. The
gargoylz had dashed off to play with
their new friends, the Barebones Brigade,
and the boys didn't want to miss out on
the fun.

"We'd better let our mums know first,"
said Max.

"I suppose so," agreed Ben. "Mums are
so silly. Always wanting to know where
we are."

They dashed around the castle grounds,
where old-fashioned stalls were selling

all sorts of things, from ye olde cider to witches' potions. They finally found their mums happily sniffing at medieval face creams.

"We're popping back inside the castle," said Max, holding his nose in disgust at the flowery smell. "We're going to study all the ancient carvings."

"Study?" said his mum, going pale with shock.

"Just be back here at five o'clock on the dot," said Ben's mum as she smeared some green paste on her cheek.

"Time to use our Special Agent Running Devices – codename: Feet," said Max.

The boys charged across the drawbridge and, after a quick detour to replace the plastic apples on the banquet

table, dashed up the winding stairs to the
battlements.

At first the roof seemed
completely empty. Then the
boys heard a growly purr.

"It's all right,
everyone. It's Max and
Ben." Toby popped out
from behind a tower.

"Why were you
hiding?" asked Max.

"There have been
humanz up here," said
Neb, suddenly
becoming visible.

Rufus and Barney appeared from over
the battlements too.

"We had our tummies poked by a
crowd of children," said Rufus.

"And two old ladies who were so tired
after the climb, they leaned on us for
ages," complained Neb.

"One rested her handbag on my head!" said Barney.

"I'll stop any more humans coming here," said Max with a grin. He picked up the **CLOSED FOR CLEANING** sign, hung it on the tower door and shut it. "Now we'll have the battlements all to ourselves."

"Hail, humanz!" came a voice.

Max's spy radar was ready: stone-coloured skin, feet and tail of a lion, piercing eyes. He knew what that meant. It was Ethelstan, commonly known as Stan, codename: Castle Gargoyle.

Stan hopped over the wall, followed by Bert, Wolf and the rest of the Barebones Brigade.

"Tell the boyz about that game you used to play," said Toby, flapping his wings in excitement. "The one called Knock-down Henry."

"When King Henry the Eighth stayed here, he liked walking by the moat with his wife—" began Stan.

"A different wife each time he came," put in Wolf.

"We used to steal bread rollz out of the kitchen and throw them at him!" Bert went on.

"Cool!" exclaimed Max, wide-eyed.

"We scored points if we knocked him over," said Stan. "And double points if we hit a wife too."

Wolf gave a huge guffaw of laughter. "A hundred points if they fell in the water!"

Stan nodded.

"It was a merry jape."

"Except for the time we nearly got caught by his guardz," added Bert. "We had to swallow all the bread in one gulp."

"I couldn't eat for days afterwardz," said Wolf. "But it was worth it."

"What a great trick," gasped Ben.

Max laughed. "A king-sized trick! You'd have had your heads chopped off if he'd caught you."

"It was most exciting," agreed Stan. "But my favourite jest was Pig in a Wig."

"When Queen Victoria came to stay, we got the fattest porker from the castle farm," explained Bert, "and we put it in the queen's bed with a wig on its head."

"When she came in, the pig gave a great snort," Wolf carried on, "and the queen was so scared she jumped out of the window and landed on the compost heap. Then lots of people rushed in and chased the pig all over the castle."

"Let's play it now," said Rufus. "I'll be the pig. But I need a wig if I'm going to give a good performance."

Neb ran off down the steps. He was soon back holding a ball of bright-yellow wool. "I couldn't find any wigs," he said, "so I borrowed this from ye olde knitting stall."

"Perfect," said Ben, scrunching up the wool and plonking it on Rufus's head.

"Barney, you can be the queen," said Max, "and find Rufus the pig in your bed. Then the rest of us will rush in and chase Rufus around the battlements."

"What a splendid idea!" declared Stan, and his friends clapped eagerly. "We never thought of acting out our adventures before."

The Barebones Brigade tiptoed around the roof, with Rufus the pig following behind, oinking loudly. They pretended to climb the spiral staircase to the queen's bedroom, then tucked him up in a pretend bed – a piece of old sacking in the corner of the battlements – and tiptoed away.

Barney mimed opening the bedroom door. "Who is that in the royal bed?" he called in a high-pitched voice, creeping towards the sleeping pig.

Rufus gave a loud **snort**! and Barney let out a deafening yell and pretended to jump out of the window. Ben, Max and the rest of the gargoylz charged up and chased Rufus around the roof.

At last they all collapsed in a heap.

"I like you, castle gargoylz," panted Barney happily. "I hope we can come and see you again."

"Of course we can," said Max. "And we've still got hours . . ." He looked at his watch. "Oh, no," he gasped. "It's nearly five o'clock. We've got to go home."

He turned to Stan. "It's been an awesome afternoon."

"Do you *have* to go?" asked the old gargoyle, his mouth turning down at the corners. "We have had such fun with you all."

His stony friends began to grumble.

"We'll come back and see you again," promised Ben.

Stan and the other castle gargoylz huddled together, muttering. Then they made a circle around their visitors.

"You humanz can depart," announced Stan. "But the Saint Mark's gargoylz must stay here with us. They can show us such good games."

"True," said Wolf. "We have not had so much fun since Bert put a kipper inside King Stephen's crown and he was followed by all the castle cats."

"Spluttering gutterz!" gasped Toby. "We can't stay here. The vicar will miss us."

Stan and his friends turned to each other and then began to talk secretly again. At last Stan held up a hand. "It is decided," he said at last. "You can all go ..."

Max and Ben sighed with relief and started towards the tower door.

". . . except Toby!" Stan went on, rubbing his paws together in glee. "He can stay here. Your vicar won't miss one little gargoyle."

With that, the castle gargoylz advanced on Toby, whose monkey face puckered up with fear.

But before he could escape, Wolf ran over with a banner and wrapped it around him tightly. Toby was trapped.

"You can't keep him here if he doesn't want to stay," protested Max.

"Why not?" said Stan with a puzzled frown. "The humanz who used to live here were always taking prisonerz."

"What are we going to do?" Ben whispered to Max. "Our mums will go mad if we're late back to the car, but we can't leave Toby."

An idea bounced into Max's brain. "Don't worry, Agent Neal," he whispered back. "I've just thought of a secret plan."

He walked over to the Barebones Brigade, who were closely guarding poor little Toby. "You win," he said loudly. "After all, we have lots of other gargoylz to play with."

He bent down to peer through Bert's legs at Toby, whose horrified face was just visible peeping out of the banner. His monkey ears were drooping sadly. Making sure no one else could see, Max gave Toby a wink. At once Toby's golden eyes lit up with relief.

"Bye then," called Max casually. He marched over to the tower door. "Come on, you lot," he called to Barney, Neb and Rufus. "We haven't got all day!"

The three little gargoylz looked horror-struck at the thought of leaving their friend, but Ben hurried them towards the spiral stairs and slammed the door behind him.

Barney turned to Max, the spines

down his back
quivering
angrily. "We
can't leave
Toby!" he
yelled. Neb
and Rufus
nodded fiercely
in agreement.

"Don't worry," said
Max quickly. "Toby will be coming home
with us."

"But he's surrounded by ferocious
gargoylz," cried Barney. "What can we
do?"

"I could turn into a skeleton," suggested
Rufus, "but I don't think they'd be scared.
They're tough old things."

"It's your secret power we need, Neb,"
said Max. "Blend into the background so
Stan and the others can't see you, then slip
across to Toby and set him free."

"Good plan, Agent Black!" exclaimed
Ben.

He opened the tower door a crack,
and Neb slipped through. Immediately
he turned the same colour as the stone
battlements. Peering through the tiny gap
in the door, Max and Ben could see the
castle gargoylz in a noisy huddle again.
Now and again they would glance over
at Toby, who was trussed up in the
far corner.

"They're arguing about what games to play with him," said Rufus.

"Can anyone see Neb?" asked Ben.

"I think he's creeping along by the battlements," said Barney.

They saw a flicker, and the faint outline of a gargoyle passed across in front of a red and gold banner. Another flicker, and Neb had blended in with the battlements again.

"I hope they don't spot him," said Rufus anxiously.

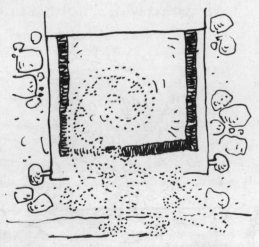

"They'll probably keep Neb as well if they do," wailed Barney, peeping through his claws.

"I can't see him at all," said Max.

"That's good," said Ben. "Then the Barebones Brigade won't see him either. Wait ... something's happening."

Toby was wriggling and writhing, a huge grin on his face.

"I just caught a glimpse of Neb," said Rufus in excitement. "He's reached Toby."

Toby suddenly let out a huge guffaw of laughter.

"Neb's supposed to be untying him," whispered Max, "not tickling him!"

The castle gargoylz stopped arguing and swung round to stare at the little monkey-faced gargoyle, who was writhing around in his banner.

"Don't worry about me!" said Toby quickly. "I'm just excited about playing gamez with you."

"Then we must agree on what we are going to play," said Stan. "Come, Barebonez Brigade. No more arguments!" They put their heads together again just

as the banner fell away from Toby.

"He's free!" cried Max.

At Max's shout, Bert looked up. "He is escaping!" he yelled.

Neb was so frightened he forgot to keep his camouflage and appeared next to Toby.

"There are two of them!" cried Stan.

"Catch them both!"

The Barebones Brigade flung themselves at Toby and Neb. Max and Ben gasped in horror. Their plan had failed, and now *two* of their friends were about to be taken prisoner!

The castle gargoylz landed in a heap, flailing about and yelling at the tops of their voices.

"Where are they?"

"Have you got them?"

"Get your foot out of my ear!"

And then the boys spotted Toby. The little gargoyle rose up out of the middle of the fray; his wings were flapping madly and Neb was dangling from his claws.

"Toby's using his special power!" cried Max.

"Do not let them go!" shouted Bert. He leaped up to grab Neb's feet, but Toby was too fast for him.

He swooped over the heads of the Barebones Brigade, keeping safely out of reach.

"Everyone's safe," exclaimed Barney, making for the stairs. "Time we were off!"

"Not yet," said Max, pointing at the Barebones Brigade, who were wailing and beating their chests. "We have to cheer the castle gargoylz up before we go."

Ben turned to Barney and Rufus. "You'd better stay here behind the door where it's safe."

"I knew we shouldn't have trusted humanz," Stan sighed when he saw the boys approaching.

"Who can we play with now?" cried Wolf, twisting his paws together in despair. "We've had such a good time today. We shall never be able to think of such wonderful gamez on our own."

"You can play tricks!" declared Ben. "That's what gargoylz do."

"But who will we play tricks on?" asked Stan. "The castle has not been the same since all the kingz and queenz left."

"You don't need kings and queens to

play tricks on," said Ben. He looked over
the battlements at all the tourists milling
around below. "You've got a whole
castle full of visitors!"

Wolf scratched his
stony helmet. "We didn't always play
tricks on kingz and queenz," he said.
"Remember when we mixed up Lord
Fatbelly's armour so that he put it on
back to front?"

"And when we put pepper in Lady

Agatha's purse and she sneezed her false teeth out," said Bert, getting excited. "We could do that sort of thing to the visitorz."

"Come together, brigade," commanded Stan. "We have jests to plot."

As the castle gargoylz scuttled across to join him, he turned to the boys with a grin. "When I saw Toby fly, it stirred something in my memory," he told them.

"Aye, me too," said Wolf. "Did we not have secret powerz once?"

"It has been so long, I have forgotten what I can do," added Bert.

"I'm sure you can remember if you think hard," said Ben. "Then you'll be able to play really awesome tricks."

"And we'll keep our promise and come
and see you again," said Max.

Toby and Neb flew down and ran
over to the tower door. Barney and Rufus
hugged them.

They left their new friends chatting
about putting ink in the bath water and
filling the keyholes with pastry.

Mrs Black and Mrs Neal were stacking their big jars of face cream in the boot when the boys reached the car. The gargoylz hid in a nearby holly bush.

"How are we going to smuggle our friends in, Agent Neal?" hissed Max. "They'll be seen."

"Leave it to me, Agent Black," Ben hissed back. He ran up to his mum. "We'll do that for you," he said sweetly, taking the heavy load.

"Oh, er, thank you," she said, looking amazed.

"That's the second time today we've been helpful," Max whispered as their mothers got into the front of the car.

"I'm beginning to feel weak!"

"Me too," replied Ben. "We'll have to get our strength up by eating all the picnic leftovers on the way home."

The boys waved at the bush.

The gargoylz rushed over, jumped into the car and all rolled themselves up in the picnic rug.

"Time for a nap," came Toby's growly purr.

"We heard some great ghost stories

from one of the guides at the castle," said Max's mum as she started the car. "Hundreds of years ago, the castle was haunted by mischievous ghosts. They put pepper in ladies' purses and even hid a fish in the king's crown!"

Arabella gave a squeal of fright. "It must have been the ghosts of the wardrobe," she quavered.

"Ghosts of the wardrobe!" squeaked Jessica-the-Echo.

"Don't worry, girls," said Mrs Neal. "The guide said there are no ghosts around any more."

"It was probably a draught making those clothes move," added Mrs Black.

The boys heard a faint chuckle from the picnic blanket.

"Something tells me there's soon going

to be some new ghost stories at Barebones
Castle," Ben whispered to Max.

"That's what happens when there's
gargoylz around," Max whispered back.
"Fantastic fun."

"*Spook*tacular fun," agreed Ben.

Gargoylz Fact File

Full name: Tobias the Third
Known as: Toby
Special Power: Flying
Likes: All kinds of pranks and mischief – especially playing jokes on the vicar
Dislikes: Mrs Hogsbottom, garden gnomes

Full name: Barnabas
Known as: Barney
Special Power: Making big stinks!
Likes: Cookiez
Dislikes: Being surprised by humanz

Full name: Eli
Special Power: Turning into a grass snake
Likes: Sssports Day, Ssslithering
Dislikes: Ssscary sssstories

Full name: Theophilus
Known as: Theo
Special Power: Turning into a ferocious tiger (well, tabby kitten!)
Likes: Sunny spots and cosy places
Dislikes: Rain

Full name: Bartholomew
Known as: Bart
Special Power: Burping spiders

Likes: Being grumpy
Dislikes: Being told to cheer up

Full name: Nebuchadnezzar
Known as: Neb
Special Power: Changing colour
to match his background
Likes: Snorkelling
Dislikes: Anyone treading on his tail

Full name: Zackary
Known as: Zack
Special Power: Making himself
invisible to humanz

Likes: Bouncing around, eating bramblz,
thistlz, and anything with Pricklz!

Dislikes: Keeping still

Name: Azzan
Special Power: Breathing fire

Likes: Surprises

Dislikes: Smoke going up his
nose and making him sneeze

Full name: Jehieli
Known as: Jelly
Special Power: Turning to jelly
Likes: Having friendz to play with
Dislikes: Bulliez and spoilsports

Name: Ira
Special Power: Making it rain
Likes: Making humanz walk the plank
Dislikes: Being bored

Name: Cyrus
Special Power: Singing lullabies to send humanz to sleep
Likes: Fun dayz out
Dislikes: Snoring

Name: Rufus
Special Power: Turning into a skeleton
Likes: Playing spooky tricks
Dislikes: Squeezing into small spaces